157082

P9-BYE-478

*
157082

Mother Makes a Mistake

Gareth Stevens Children's Books
MILWAUKEE

To Marguerite Turner
my most special mother
                    A. D.

For Ilze, Ian and Esther
                    E. A.

**For a free color catalog describing Gareth Stevens' list of
high-quality books, call 1-800-542-2595 (USA)
or 1-800-461-9120 (Canada). Gareth Stevens' Fax: (414) 225-0377.**

Library of Congress Cataloging-in-Publication Data

Dorer, Ann.
    Mother makes a mistake / by Ann Dorer.
        p. cm.
    Summary: Knowing Kate would rather play than bathe,
Mother mistakes the word for bath, substituting other words
so many times, Kate finally insists on being given a bath.
    ISBN 0-8368-0109-1
    [1. Baths—Fiction.] I. Title.
PZ7.D72745Mo 1989
[E]—dc20   89-42638

A Gareth Stevens Publishing edition

Edited, designed, and produced by
Gareth Stevens Publishing
1555 North RiverCenter Drive, Suite 201
Milwaukee, Wisconsin 53212, USA

Text © 1991 by Ann Dorer
Illustrations © 1991 by Gareth Stevens, Inc.
Format © 1991 by Gareth Stevens, Inc.

Designer: Kate Kriege

Printed in the United States of America

4 5 6 7 8 9 99 98 97 96 95 94

Mother
Makes a
Mistake

Written by Ann Dorer

Illustrated by Ellen Anderson

It was a tired time of day. Kate was busy coloring at the kitchen table, and Mother was busy cleaning up the kitchen.

Finally, Mother turned the knob on the dishwasher, and the supper dishes began to slush and bump.

4

Mother smiled at Kate. "Well, now that the dishes are getting clean, there is a little person around here who needs to get clean, too. I wonder who she is."

Kate kept coloring.

"Kate," Mother said, "don't you think it's time to . . ."

A frown crossed Kate's face.

Mother began again. "Kate, you got so dirty playing outside today. We really do need to put you in the . . .

. . . bottle."

Kate looked up.
"The bottle?"

Mother laughed. "I am tired,"
she said. "I made a mistake.
I didn't mean to say 'bottle.'
I meant to say that it's time to
put you in the . . .

11

. . . bucket."

"Bucket?" asked Kate.
"I wouldn't fit in a bucket!"

"Oh, no!" said Mother. "Did I say 'bucket'?
Only your feet would fit in a bucket. I should
have said that it's time to put you in the . . .

13

. . . bouquet."

"Momma," said Kate, "I don't belong in a bunch of flowers!"

"They might make you smell a little better,"
said Mother, "but you are right. A bouquet
is not where I need to put you. I really need
to put you in the . . .

. . . bacon bits."

"Bacon bits?" said Kate.
"Do I look like a salad?"

"Your hair is a little tossed," answered Mother, "but no, you don't look like a salad. Come with me and we'll put you where you belong — right in the . . .

. . . blueberry bush."

"You are going to put me in the
blueberry bush?" asked Kate.

"Of course not," said Mother. "I don't want a blue you. I think I am getting a little mixed-up. Where I really need to put you is in the . . .

19

. . . basketball net."

"I think you are getting a **lot** mixed-up," said Kate.

"Let me concentrate very hard," Mother said. "Now, my little daughter is dirty, and I need to put her somewhere to get her clean. Just exactly where should I put her? Maybe I should put her in the . . .

21

. . .bus," said Mother.

"No," said Kate.

"In the begonias?"
asked Mother.

"No, no," said Kate.

"In the balloon?" asked Mother.

"No, no, no," said Kate.

"How about the baking-powder biscuits?"

"No, no, no, no, no!" answered Kate.

"Not even with blackberry jelly on them?"

"No," answered Kate.

"Well, I absolutely, completely, totally give up," said Mother. "Where am I supposed to put you, Kate?"

"You are supposed to put me in the **BATHTUB!**" explained Kate.

"Are you sure?" asked Mother.

"Yes," said Kate.

"Do I have to?" asked Mother.

"Yes," answered Kate.

"Well, if you say I have to, then I guess I have to," said Mother.

Mother ran Kate's bath water
as Kate undressed.

Kate climbed into the bathtub and sat
in the warm water.

29

"You are right, Kate. This is the perfect place to get you clean," said Mother.

Mother dipped the washcloth into the water, spread it over her hand, and pointed to the soap dish. "Now, will you please hand me the . . .

. . . sock?"